Small Stories

PHILIP C. STEAD

A NEAL PORTER BOOK
ROARING BROOK PRESS
NEW YORK

To Christian

A Neal Porter Book
Published by Roaring Brook Press
Roaring Brook Press is a division of Holtzbrinck Publishing Holdings Limited Partnership
175 Fifth Avenue, New York, NY 10010
The artwork for this book was handmade using gouache, water-soluble crayon, chalk pastel, and charcoal.
mackids.com

Library of Congress Control Number: 2017957307
ISBN: 978-1-62672-655-0

Our books may be purchased in bulk for promotional, educational, or business use. Please contact your local bookseller or the Macmillan Corporate and Premium Sales Department at (800) 221-7945 ext. 5442 or by e-mail at MacmillanSpecialMarkets@macmillan.com.

First edition, 2018
Book design by Philip C. Stead
Printed in China by RR Donnelley Asia Printing Solutions Ltd., Dongguan City, Guangdong Province
1 3 5 7 9 10 8 6 4 2

CONTENTS

Vernon is waiting.

Vernon is still waiting.
He has been waiting for a very long time.

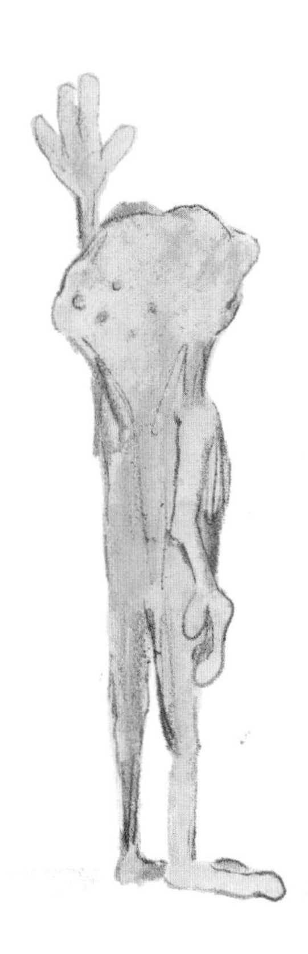

Vernon waits, and waits, and waits.
Vernon wonders if he will ever not be waiting.

Vernon is on his way.

FISHING

Vernon, Skunk, and Porcupine went out for a morning walk.

"It is a very nice day," said Vernon.

Porcupine agreed. "I do not remember a day a nice as this."

"Except for maybe yesterday," offered Skunk.

Then the three friends walked some more, enjoying the very nice day.

When the walk was finished they sat down.
"What should we do now?" asked Skunk.
"We could go for a walk," suggested Porcupine.
"Or," said Vernon, "we could go fishing."
"I would like to go fishing," said Skunk.
Porcupine said nothing.

He did not know how to fish.

"We will start by eating lunch," said Vernon.
"Fishing makes me very hungry," said Skunk.
"Me too," said Porcupine.

But Porcupine was too nervous to eat.

Vernon yawned. "Next we will take a nap." He stretched out on the soft ground.

"Fishing is a lot of work," said Skunk, and he fell asleep in a hurry.

Porcupine could not sleep. “I am not good at fishing,” he worried. “I am ruining everything.”

Vernon and Skunk woke up.

"I am enjoying fishing very much," said Skunk.

"Me too," said Vernon.

Porcupine said nothing.

"I agree," said Vernon. "If all we do is talk, then we'll never finish our fishing. We should go and find a quiet place."

Vernon climbed up onto a smooth rock. "Here is good," he said. "There is room enough for everyone."

Vernon, Skunk, and Porcupine sat together. They watched the water rushing along.

"If I were a fish," said Skunk, "I would not like to be wet all the time."

Porcupine agreed. "I agree," he said.

Then Vernon, Skunk, and Porcupine thought about what it would be like to be a fish.

After a while Vernon asked, "Do fish have toes?"

"I am not sure," said Skunk.

"Sometimes," said Vernon, "I like to get my toes wet."

Then no one said anything for a while. They sat and didn't think about much.

"How long does fishing take?" asked Skunk.

"I am not sure," said Vernon.

"What do we do if we see a fish?" asked Skunk. "I have never been fishing."

"I do not know," said Vernon. "I have never been fishing either."

Porcupine spoke up. "If we see a fish," he said, "maybe we should say hello."

"That is a good idea," said Vernon.

"Yes," said Skunk. "That is a very good idea."

“HELLO!”

"Can we go fishing tomorrow?" asked Porcupine.

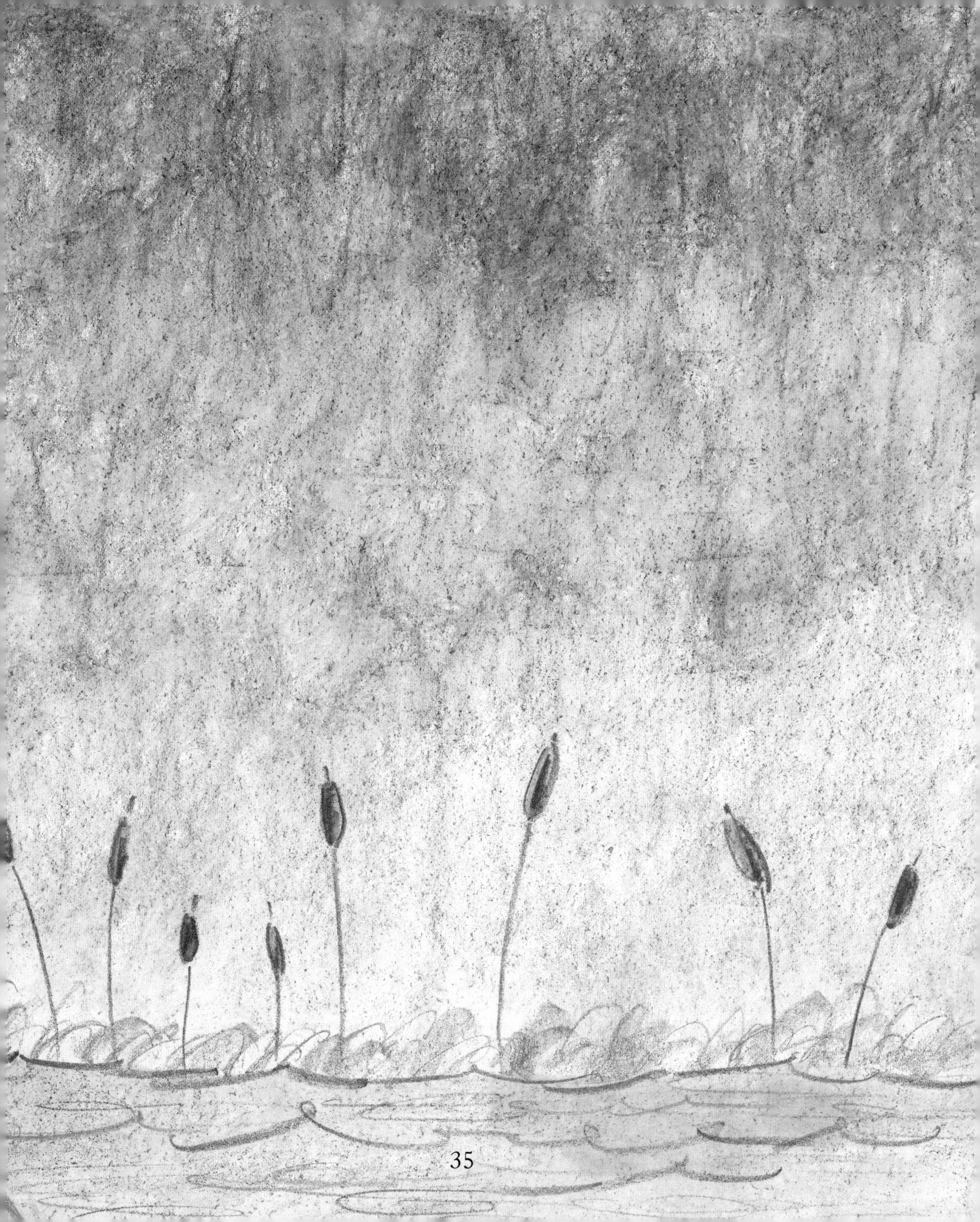

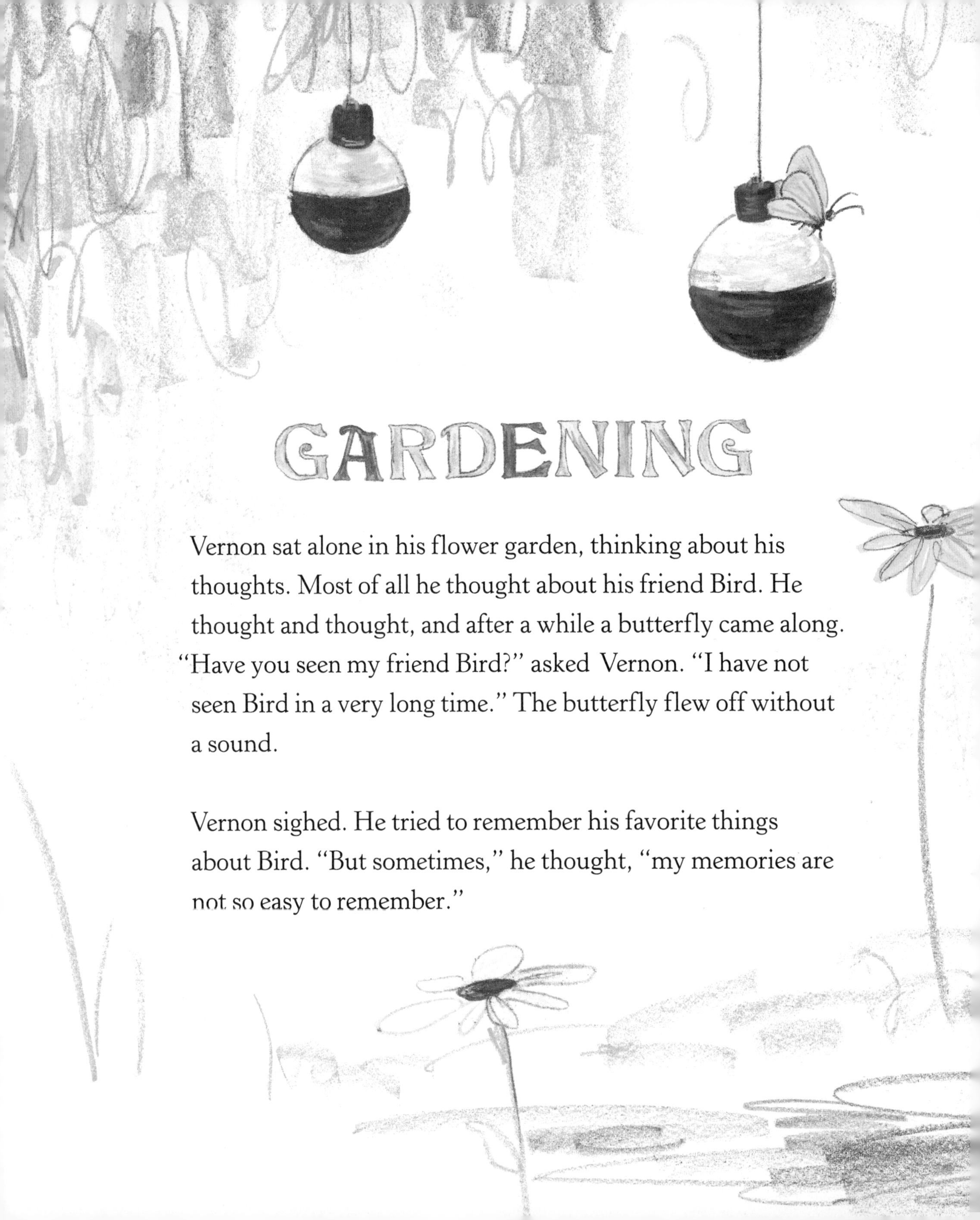

GARDENING

Vernon sat alone in his flower garden, thinking about his thoughts. Most of all he thought about his friend Bird. He thought and thought, and after a while a butterfly came along. "Have you seen my friend Bird?" asked Vernon. "I have not seen Bird in a very long time." The butterfly flew off without a sound.

Vernon sighed. He tried to remember his favorite things about Bird. "But sometimes," he thought, "my memories are not so easy to remember."

So Vernon went out to look for his memories.

"Where are you going?" asked Skunk.
"I am going to the river," said Vernon. "Because Bird liked the river."
"Oh," said Skunk. "There is a butterfly on your head."
"I don't think so," said Vernon. "But thank you."

Vernon sat by the river. "I wonder if my flowers are thirsty," he thought.

Then he carried water back for his flowers to drink.

"Where are you going?" asked Porcupine.

"I am going to the forest," said Vernon. "Because Bird liked the forest."

"Oh," said Porcupine. "There is a butterfly on your head."

"I don't think so," said Vernon. "But thank you."

Vernon explored the forest. He stopped to admire a bright blue flower. "This flower reminds me of Bird," he thought.

Then he pulled the flower up and brought it back to his garden for planting.

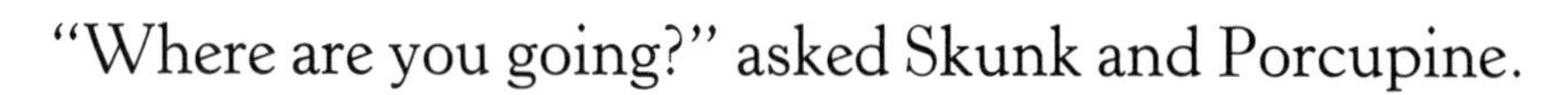

"Where are you going?" asked Skunk and Porcupine.

"I am going cloud watching," said Vernon. "Because Bird liked to watch the clouds."

"Oh," said Skunk.

"Oh," said Porcupine.

"These clouds would look nice above my garden," thought Vernon. Then he spotted a cloud that reminded him of Bird. Vernon felt happy remembering his friend. "I wish my favorite things were always nearby," he thought.

As Vernon wished he felt tired from all the walking, and the watering, and the planting, and the watching. Vernon closed his eyes and fell asleep.

"I am worried," said Skunk.

"I am worried too," said Porcupine. "There are a lot of things to worry about."

"I am worried that Vernon misses Bird," said Skunk.

"Me too," said Porcupine. "Maybe we can find something for Vernon. Something that will cheer him up."

So Skunk and Porcupine went foraging for interesting things.

They searched by the river

and rummaged through the forest floor.

"What will Vernon like?" they wondered.

They could not decide.

Soon they were back in Vernon's garden.

"We should find Vernon and apologize," said Skunk.

"I agree," said Porcupine. He had wanted to make Vernon happy.

Skunk and Porcupine waited.

“We are still waiting,” thought Skunk.
“We have been waiting for a very long time,” thought Porcupine.

Skunk and Porcupine waited, and waited, and waited.
Skunk and Porcupine wondered if they would ever not be waiting.

Then Vernon dreamed he had an itch on his nose.

And Vernon woke up.

"You brought me my garden!" he said.
"I don't think so," said Porcupine . . .

"But I'm glad you are happy."